THE MAGIC BEAN TREE
A LEGEND FROM ARGENTINA

Retold by Nancy Van Laan
Paintings by Beatriz Vidal

Houghton Mifflin Company • Boston 1998

For my dear niece, Hannah,
who will never outgrow her fondness for picture books
—N.V.L.

Pour nôtre petit poisson, Marie Eva
—B.V.

Text copyright © 1998 by Nancy Van Laan
Illustrations copyright © 1998 by Beatriz Vidal

All rights reserved. For information about permission
to reproduce selections from this book, write to Permissions,
Houghton Mifflin Company, 215 Park Avenue South,
New York, New York 10003.

The text of this book is set in 16 point Dante MT.
The illustrations are gouache, reproduced in full color.

Library of Congress Cataloging-in-Publication Data
Van Laan, Nancy
   The magic bean tree: a legend from Argentina / retold by
   Nancy Van Laan; paintings by Beatriz Vidal.
      p. cm.
Includes bibliographical references
   Summary: A young Quechuan boy sets out on his own to bring the
rains back to his parched homeland and is rewarded by a gift of
carob beans that come to be prized across Argentina.
   ISBN 0-395-82746-9
   1. Quechua Indians—Folklore. 2. Legends—Argentina.
[1. Indians of South America—Folklore. 2. Folklore—Argentina.
3. Locust trees—Folklore.] I. Vidal, Beatriz, ill. II. Title.
F2230.2.K4V367 1998   96-38632
398.2'08998323—dc20   CIP
                                        AC

Manufactured in Singapore
TWP 10 9 8 7 6 5 4 3 2 1

GLOSSARY

armadillo: A hard-shelled burrowing mammal related to the anteater. It has no teeth and is mostly nocturnal.

carob tree: (KA-rub) This tree's roots, which reach deep into the earth, can store great amounts of water, even in a drought. The Quechuan word for carob tree is *amapik* (AH-mah-pik).

Great Bird of the Underworld: Many South American Indian myths feature a large bird, often referred to as the Great Bird of the Underworld, which hides the stars behind its wings.

Life Giver: The sun god

llama: A humpless, camel-like animal that can carry heavy loads and is also highly valued among the people of the Andes region for its wool, flesh, and milk.

Mother of Storms: The bringer of rainfall

north wind: In the pampas, the north wind brings dry, hot air down from the equator.

Pachamama: Earth's mother, god of the ground, and "teacher of the world." She is an important figure to many South American Indian peoples.

pampas: A Quechuan word that means "fields without trees"—a vast flat grassland in southern South America that extends from the Atlantic coast to the Andes.

Pampero: (pahm-PAY-ro) The strong south wind of the pampas that brings heavy storm clouds and bounteous rain.

Quechua: (KECH-wa) The language of the South American Indians that originally constituted the ruling class of the Incan empire. It is now also spoken by other Indian peoples of Peru, Ecuador, Bolivia, Chile, and Argentina.

rhea: (REE-uh) A large, flightless pampas ostrich

Topec: A Quechuan name for a young boy

Underworld: A mythical region that is said to be the dwelling place of all that is evil.

SOURCES

Burland, Cottie. *Mythology of the Americas.* London: The Hamlyn Publishing Group, 1970.

Bushnell, G.H.S. *The Ancient People of the Andes.* Penguin Books, Harmondsworth, 1949.

El Indio Pampero en la Literatura Gauchesca. in *Conrado Alminaque.*

Hartt, Charles Fred. *Amazonian Tortoise Myths.* Rio de Janero, 1875.

Hudson, W. H. *South American Sketches.* London: Duckworth and Company, 1909.

Karsten, Rafael. *The Toba Indians of the Bolivian Gran Chaco.* The Netherlands: Anthropological Publications, 1970.

Roth, Walter E. "Inquiry into Animism and Folklore of the Guiana Indians," Washington, D.C.: Smithsonian Institution, *The Thirtieth Annual Report of the Bureau of American Ethnology,* 1908–09.

Steward, Julian H. *Handbook of South American Indians.* Washington, D.C.: Smithsonian Institution, Bureau of American Ethnology. Bulletin 143, Vols. 2, 5, and 6, 1946–50.

At first in the long ago time there was just one tree. In the middle of the wide pampas, this one tree stood all alone. Its ancient roots held water from the earth's first rainfall. Full of magic, the carob tree stretched toward the sky like a green umbrella.

Then came a summer when no rain fell. The waving grasses of the wide, wide pampas grew brown and still. Day after day the hot sun scorched the feet of those who walked. Even in the highlands, the streams and lakes dried up. Without water, everything would soon die.

The herders of llamas on the edge of the pampas knew this to be true. But what could they do? They had stopped praying, for the gods of the Great Sky World no longer talked. The voice of Pachamama no longer made the ground tremble or the mountains smoke. The breath of Life Giver no longer pushed stars to the night skies nor clouds to the day skies. All Life Giver hung in the sky was the sun, fierce and hot.

When no rain came, only little Topec prayed each day. He prayed to Life Giver; he prayed to Pachamama; he prayed to Pampero and Mother of Storms. When no rain came, Topec decided that the rain had lost its way.

"I will find rain," he said, "and bring it back."

Everyone worried.

"Little Topec, don't go, for you might crumble like the plants."

"Little Topec, don't go, for you might turn into dust like the earth."

But through the tall grasses Topec walked. Plants crumbled as he walked. Dust burned his eyes as he walked. Still Topec went on until he came to what was once a deep river.

"Tell me, O River, have you seen rain?"

"No rain, no rain. So dry, I will soon die," murmured the river.

"I will find rain and bring it back," promised Topec.

The river worried.

"Hide from the sun, little one. Curl up like the armadillo. Cover your head like the rhea, or you will die, too!"

But Topec went on.

He saw armadillos rolled into balls, hiding from the sun. He saw rheas with wing-covered heads, hiding from the sun. But little Topec kept walking.

Far, far from his village, Topec felt the biting sting of the hot north wind on his cheek.

"Tell me, O North Wind," he said, "have you seen rain?"

"*Hawishhhh . . .*" huffed North Wind, but he didn't answer.

Instead, his strong breath lifted Topec, swirling him in a cloud of dust across the wide pampas. Finally Topec caught on something cool, something soothing, and dropped to the ground in a deep sleep.

The next day, when the sun woke
Topec, he looked up. Why, he was under
Carob Tree, the only tree growing in the
wide pampas—and its leaves were still
moist and green!

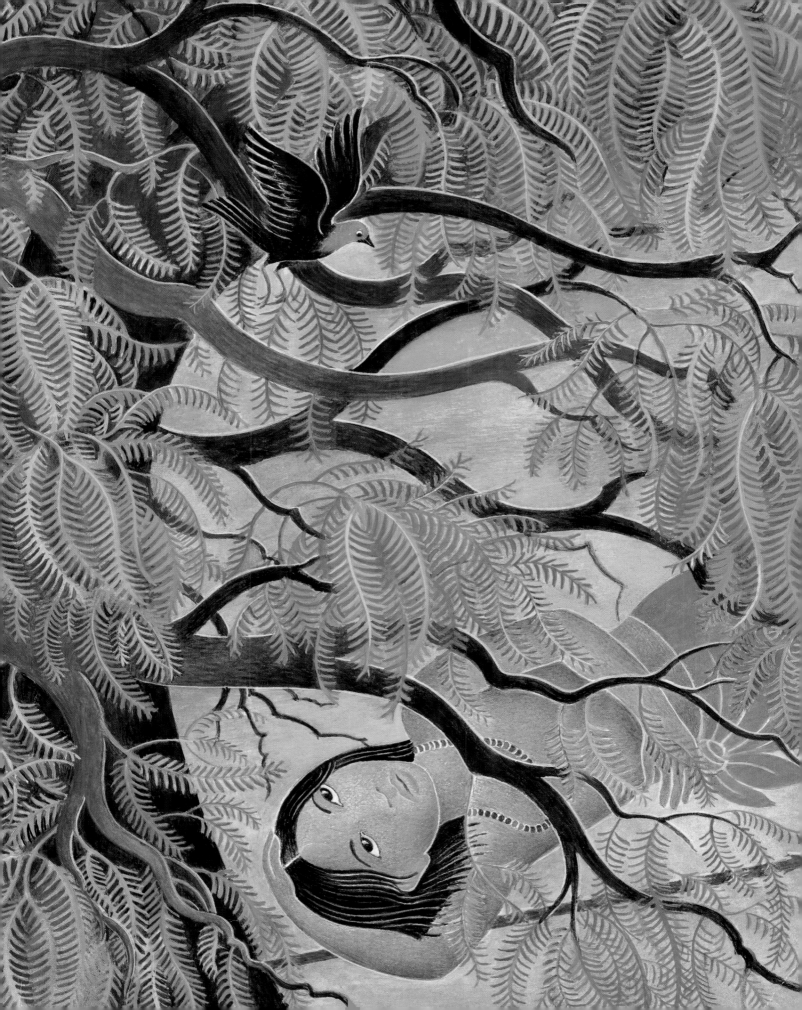

"Tell me, O Carob Tree, have you seen rain?"

"No rain, no rain," sighed the tree. "Great Bird of the Underworld is in the way."

Topec did not know who this was.

"Its wings reach from one end of the sky to the other," explained the tree. "So the gods cannot see that the pampas need rain. And they cannot hear your prayers."

"Then I shall find this evil bird and kill it!" cried Topec.

"Nothing can kill it, little one. You must make it go somewhere else."

"Very well," said Topec. "I will find a way."

"Since you are so brave," said the tree, "I shall share my secret with you."

Each night when the skies dim,
Great Bird sleeps on my highest limb.
Come back, little one, come back then,
Before the sun lights earth once again.

Quickly Topec hurried back to his village, for the words of the wise tree had given him a plan.

When darkness fell, the carob tree's words proved to be true, for settled among its branches was the Great Bird of the Underworld with its wings folded, deep in sleep.

As the thick warmth of the night skies dimmed the stars, the earth became still. Then, from the other side of the wide pampas, tiny lights suddenly appeared. It was little Topec leading the way!

With torches lit, he brought his people to where the powerful carob tree stood.

BOOM BOOMBA, BOOM BOOMBA!
The herders beat their drums, banged on sticks, rattled rattles, and raised their voices, shrieking, screaming, filling the air with such noise the earth shook.

The upper branches of the carob tree
swayed as though pushed by a sudden storm.
"Louder!" cried Topec.
BOOM BOOMBA, BOOM BOOMBA, BOOM BOOMBA!

Then, from all over the pampas animals came running,
leaping, hopping, jumping, adding their voices to those of the people.
SNORT SNORT HISS! YAP YAP YEOW!
Suddenly the Great Bird cried out, "AU-AUK! AU-AUK!"

Frightened by the sound of so many voices, the wicked bird flew out of the treetop.

"AU-AUK! AU-AUK!"

Up, up, high into the air it soared, hiding the moon behind its enormous wings. As Great Bird of the Underworld vanished beyond the night sky, a chant rose up from the people below:

> *Life Giver, see us!*
> *Pachamama, see us!*
> *Pampero, hear us!*
> *Mother of Storms, hear us!*

A low rumble sounded in the distant sky as a thick dark cloud formed. . . .

. . . And, at last, came rain!

All through the night the rain poured on the pampas, filling up its rivers and turning its brown grass green. When the sky cleared at sunrise, the mighty branches of the carob tree shook, covering the ground with golden-red beans. These were a gift for Topec, for being so brave and for finding a way to bring back the rain.

From the beans came fodder to feed the llamas. From the beans came flour to make porridge and cake. And from the seeds of the beans grew many more carob trees . . .

. . . throughout the land of Argentina.

Today the people of Argentina still tell the story of brave Topec and the magic carob tree. And they still plant its seedlings near their homes, for though it takes a carob tree a long time to grow, its shade is said to bring good luck.